Hush!

A Gaelic Lullaby

CAROLE GERBER · ILLUSTRATED BY MARTY HUSTED

WHISPERING COYOTE PRESS

Published by Whispering Coyote Press
480 Newbury Street, Suite 104, Danvers, MA 01923
Text copyright © 1997 by Carole Gerber
Illustrations copyright © 1997 by Marty Husted

10 9 8 7 6 5 4 3 2 1

Book design and production by *The Kids at Our House*
Text set in 22-point Goudy Old Style Bold

Library of Congress Cataloging–in–Publication Data

Gerber, Carole.
Hush! a Gaelic lullaby / written by Carole Gerber; illustrated by Marty Husted.
p.   cm.
Summary: A traditional Gaelic lullaby about a baby who cries until its relatives, after preparing for an impending storm, gather around it.
ISBN 1–879085–57–7
1. Children's poetry, American.   2. Family—Juvenile poetry.   [1. Ireland—Poetry.   2. Lullabies.   3. American poetry.]
I. Husted, Marty. 1957—   ill.   II. Title.
PS3557.E657HB   1997
811'.54—dc20   96–31907
                                CIP
                                AC

To Paige and Jessica
—C.G.

To Emily, who never sleeps
—M.H.

Hush! The waves are rolling in,
white with foam, white with foam.

Sister takes the washing down...

as baby cries at home.

Hush! The wind roars loud and fast.
Hear it moan. Hear it moan.

Brother gathers peat nearby...

as baby cries at home.

Hush! The sheep are frightened now.
See them roam. See them roam.

Grandpa goes to round them up . . .

as baby cries at home.

Hush! The rain beats on the leaves.
See them blown. See them blown.

Mother brings the peat inside . . .

as baby cries at home.

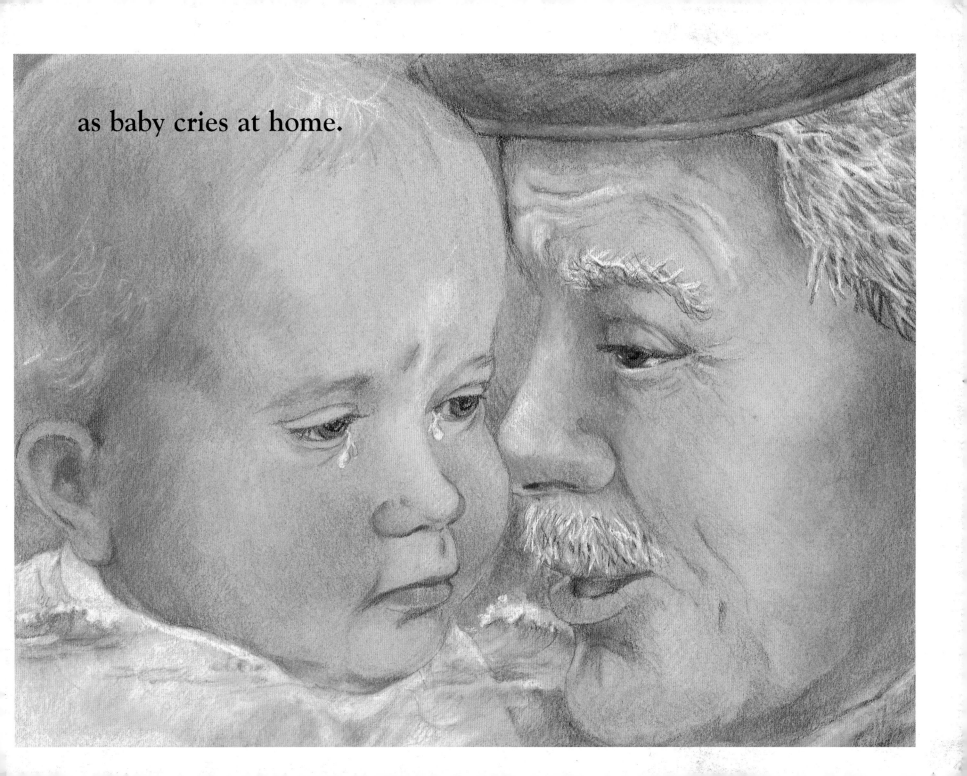

Hush! The house creaks in the storm.
Hear it groan. Hear it groan.

Father fastens shutters tight . . .

as baby cries at home.

Hush! The room is gray and cold.
Cold as stone. Cold as stone.

Grandma builds a crackling fire...

as baby cries at home.

Hush! Six voices talking now.
Hear their tones. Hear their tones.

The family gathers
close around . . .

as baby sleeps at home.

Hush! A Gaelic Lullaby is loosely based on an ancient song in Gaelic, the official language of Ireland.